CAPTAIN AWESOME

VS. THE SINISTER SUBSTITUTE TEACHER

By STAN KIRBY

Illustrated by GEORGE O'CONNOR

LITTLE SIMON

New York London Toronto Sydney New Delhi

This book is a work of fiction. Any references to historical events, real people, or real places are used fictitiously. Other names, characters, places, and events are products of the author's imagination, and any resemblance to actual events or places or persons, living or dead, is entirely coincidental.

LITTLE SIMON

An imprint of Simon & Schuster Children's Publishing Division • 1230 Avenue of the Americas, New York, New York 10020 • First Little Simon paperback edition March 2016. Copyright © 2016 by Simon & Schuster, Inc. All rights reserved, including the right of reproduction in whole or in part in any form. LITTLE SIMON is a registered trademark of Simon & Schuster, Inc., and associated colophon is a trademark of Simon & Schuster, Inc. For information about special discounts for bulk purchases, please contact Simon & Schuster Special Sales at 1-866-506-1949 or business@simonandschuster.com. The Simon & Schuster Speakers Bureau can bring authors to your live event. For more information or to book an event contact the Simon & Schuster Speakers Bureau at 1-866-248-3049 or visit our website at www.simonspeakers.com. Designed by Jay Colvin. The text of this book was set in Little Simon Gazette.

Manufactured in the United States of America 0116 FFG 10 9 8 7 6 5 4 3 2 1

Cataloging-in-Publication Data for this title is available from the Library of Congress.

ISBN 978-1-4814-5859-7 (hc)

ISBN 978-1-4814-5858-0 (pbk)

ISBN 978-1-4814-5860-3 (eBook)

Table of Contents

CHAPTER I

Good-bye, Weekend. Hello, Homework

By Eugene

Worst day of the week?" Captain Awesome asked the Sunnyview Superhero Squad. The team had gathered at its top-secret headquarters in the tree at Captain Awesome's house. The other two members of the squad, Nacho Cheese Man and Supersonic Sal, raised their hands.

Nacho Cheese Man said, "Any day I run out of spray cheese and

have to fight evil the old fashioned way. With cheese *slices*."

Super-sonic Sal, the fastest superhero in Sunnyview, said, "Wednesday."

"Hmmmm, why Wednesday?" Captain Awesome asked.

"Because Tuesday and Thursday are my piano lesson days, and Wednesday isn't," Sal replied.

But Captain Awesome knew what the *real* worst day was. "It's Sunday," he said. "Sunday is the last day of the weekend, and our crime fighting stops since we have to go to school."

"But crime fighting never stops," Supersonic Sal pointed out.

Captain Awesome thought about this and shrugged. "You're right," he replied. "But we can't do as *much* crime fighting during the school week."

"But what about Dr. Yuck Spinach and the Evil Crosswalk Orange Vestman? And worst of all, Little Miss Stinky Pinky?" Supersonic Sal said. "We have to fight those villains every day!"

"Well, we did do a lot of evil-fighting this weekend," Nacho Cheese Man added. "I have the list right here!" He held up his cheesebook, a cheese-colored notebook that even had spots of green mold on it.

"Cheesebook Checklist Check-Off!" yelled Captain Awesome.

"We built a mighty Fortress of Protection in the backyard," Nacho Cheese Man called out.

"And we patrolled the neighborhood on our Non-Subatomic Pedaling Machines," Supersonic Sal said.

"And we closed the latch on Ms. Vallance's gate so her dogs wouldn't run away," Nacho Cheese Man added.

"Right! And we put the lids back on Mr. Tootsnoot's trash cans to keep them safe from Boom-Boom Raccoon," Captain Awesome said. "Super Dude would be proud of the Sunnyview Superhero Squad!"

What? What's that you say?!

You've never heard of Super Dude? Do you live in a meadow of unicorns and chase rainbows with cotton candy buckets?

Super Dude is the star of the greatest comic book series, the best TV show in the world, and the best video game ever! He once Dude-punched the Electric Eve-Eel

so hard it was under-sea lights out! More importantly, he's the reason that Eugene McGillicudy, Charlie Thomas Jones, and Sally Williams became Sunnyview's own superheroes! But even Super

Dude can't stop the weekend from ending.

"Roly poly moley!" Captain Awesome suddenly cried out. "My Awesome Sense of Smell is smelling something . . . awful!"

PEW!

Down below, Queen Stinky-pants, who often dis-guised herself as Eugene's baby sis-ter, had just raced out from his house.

Eugene's dad ran after her. "Stop her!" he yelled. "It's a Stage Four diaper disaster!"

"Sunnyview Superhero Squad, it's time to get MI-TEE!" Captain Awesome cried. The trio quickly—but carefully—climbed down the tree-house ladder.

"CHEESY YO!" Nacho Cheese Man

shot a blast of pepper jack across the lawn. Queen Stinkypants turned to avoid it.

"SPEEDY GO!" Supersonic Sal ran toward the baby villain. Captain Awesome saw his chance. With two super leaps and a bound, he ran across the yard. Queen Stinkypants zigged, then zagged. But Captain Awesome was close behind.

"I've got you, Queen Stinky—"

"Look out!" Eugene's dad cried.

Too late.

BLAST!

POOT-POOT!

"Argh!" Captain Awesome cried out. His eyes watered. His throat burned. A cloud of stink the size of an alien battle cruiser filled the yard.

"It's the dreaded Fog of Stinkydoom," Nacho Cheese Man said, pinching his nose.

Supersonic Sal skidded to a stop. "That's a mega Pee-Yew."

There was no time to lose. "Activate Awesome Vision Power." Captain Awesome snapped his goggles over his eyes and waved his arms to clear away the stink.

Through the gross fog he saw the one thing that could stop Queen

Stinkypants: her stuffed henchdoll with the curly hair and red dress.

Captain Awesome grabbed it with two fingers so it wouldn't spread nasty stink-germs to his whole hand.

"Behold! Your doll of awfulness, Queen Stinkypants," said Captain Awesome.

She ran toward him, her stinky arms reaching for the minion.

"Now!" Captain Awesome said.

Eugene's dad swooped out of the fog and scooped her up.

Queen Stinkypants giggled. "Thanks, Captain," Eugene's dad said. "Couldn't have done it without your help. Now don't forget to do your homework. Tomorrow's Monday."

HOMEWORK! ARGH!

"At least Ms. Beasley's a good teacher and doesn't give us *too* much work," Nacho Cheese Man told Captain Awesome.

"All good superheroes do their homework," Supersonic Sal added.

Just then, Charlie's mom arrived to take him and Sally home.

"See you guys at school tomorrow." Captain Awesome took off his goggles and headed to the house, where his math homework was waiting to be conquered.

CHAPTER 2

Doom . . .
Mr. Dooms

By
Eugene

No Mr. Drools attacking from the left," Charlie noted.

"The Sewer Slammer is safely underground," Sally added.

"And Fly High McDanger isn't dropping his cloud bombs from the air," Eugene said. "We are a go for school. Let's hit the crosswalk." The friends walked safely across the street and into Sunnyview Elementary.

The hallways were also clear, and they entered Ms. Beasley's classroom without a problem.

Or so they thought.

"Well, if it isn't Puke-Gene and the Sunnyview Super-Pukies!"

Ugh. Her.

"Hello, My! Me! Mine! Meredith," Eugene said.

Meredith Mooney was the pinkest girl in class. Perhaps even the world. With her matching pink shoes, pink dress, pink shirt, and pink ribbon in her hair, she looked like an evil pink troll doll. When she wasn't busy being just plain annoying Meredith, she was also Captain Awesome's archenemy, Little Miss Stinky Pinky.

Meredith put her arm around Eugene and noogied his head. She laughed. Then her smile disap-

peared. "I'll be watching you." She pointed two fingers to her eyes, then pointed at Eugene, then back to her eyes. "That's right, you. Me. Watching you."

Meredith skipped to her cubby and put away her backpack.

"She's up to something pink," Sally said.

"She's *always* up to something pink," Charlie said. "Watching her

watching us watching her watching—wait, I've lost count."

"We'll be watching her," Eugene
said. "But first, did you hear that?"

"I don't hear anything," said
Charlie.

"That's the point," said Eugene.
"Shouldn't Ms. Beasley be telling
us to sit down now?"

"Ohhh," Charlie ohhhed.

"Where is Ms. Beasley?" Sally asked.

"She's never late," Eugene added.

The bell rang. The kids waited. Still no Ms. Beasley.

"Maybe she's at the robot lab getting a giant mechanical arm or

a bionic eye that can see through walls!" Charlie said hopefully.

The classroom door slowly opened. The morning sun streamed through the window. The mysterious figure in the doorway was just a silhouette.

SHOCK! HORROR!

That's not Ms. Beasley! Eugene thought. *Not at all!*

The doorway stranger cleared his throat. "Greetings, everyone!" the voice boomed. The whole classroom vibrated.

"My name is . . . Mr. Dooms," he boomed. His voice sounded like it could take the paint off a bicycle. He was tall and thin, with wire-rim glasses and curly black hair. "I'll be your substitute teacher for a few days."

SUBSTITUTE?

The class buzzed like bees in a honeycomb.

Mr. Dooms chuckled. "Don't worry, class. Ms. Beasley is visiting her family in New Jersey, and she'll be back next week."

Eugene turned to his friends. "Ms. Beasley has never said anything about family or New Jersey before."

"Something stinks like Queen Stinkypants on a hot day, guys," Sally said.

"Could it be my double jalapeño spray cheese?" Charlie sniffed the can in his desk. "Nope. All good."

"Let's get the day started, class," Mr. Dooms boomed. "Pop quiz!"

Pop quiz? Ms. Beasley would never give a pop quiz on a Monday. Never. *Something's definitely up with this sub guy,* Eugene thought.

"Looks like we have someone *else* to watch

now," he whispered to Charlie.

"I've already written his name down in my cheesebook," Charlie said with a nod.

CHAPTER 3

Where's Ms. Beasley?

By Eugene

Things were very different when I was in second grade . . ." Mr. Dooms began.

YAWN.

I'd rather be fighting Captain Plantain and his Banana Baddies, Eugene thought. *Where is Ms. Beasley?*

The Sunnyview Superhero Squad was keeping an eye on the substitute.

As far as being evil went, he did not disappoint.

Mr. Dooms filled the day with three bad-guy things:

He forgot all about snack time!

He forgot all about recess!

He told that story about the phone. Again.

"I hope this is the last we've seen of Mr. Dooms," Sally said when the final bell rang, ending the school day.

"That would be mi-tee times a bazillion," Eugene agreed. "There's only so much doom we can take. Let's hope Ms. Beasley is back tomorrow."

But Ms. Beasley did not return the next day.

Mr. Dooms did.

"We're going to have to take matters into our own hands," Eugene said at lunch that day. "First, let's see if he's a robot."

"I've got this." Charlie raised his hand. "Mr. Dooms, are you a robot?"

Mr. Dooms chuckled.

"No, I'm not a robot, although that reminds me of a story—"

Here we go again, Eugene thought.

On the third day, Ms. Beasley still did not return. It was like New Jersey had eaten her and wasn't going to spit her back out.

At least Mr. Dooms didn't forget recess again.

RING!

The class shot out the

door. Eugene, Charlie, and Sally stayed behind, pretending to look through their cubbies.

"Don't forget to get some fresh air, kids," Mr. Dooms said. Then he left to go wherever it is evil substitute teachers go during recess.

"Charlie, watch the door," Sally said as soon as Mr. Dooms left.

"Watch it do what?" Charlie asked.

"Just keep an eye on the hallway and let us know when he's coming back," Eugene said.

"On it!" Charlie gave a salute.

While Mr. Dooms was gone, Eugene and Sally looked through Ms. Beasley's desk and chair for secret notes, a map, or a list that read, "Places to Search for Teachers."

"Got anything yet?" Eugene asked.

"A paper clip in the shape of a big *S* and a really old candy bar. You?"

"I found a Post-it note with a doodle. It could be a map to Mr. Dooms's evil base of badness," Eugene said. "Or a duck."

Suddenly, Charlie burst back into the room. "He's coming!"

Eugene and Sally frantically cleaned up the desk, and then slipped outside with Charlie.

"What do we do now, Eugene?" Sally asked once they were outside.

"Recess, of course," Eugene replied. "We've still got three minutes left. Let's hit the swings!"

CHAPTER 4

The Teacher of No Return

By
Eugene

This New Jersey story sounds fishier than Commander Whale Shark's Tuna Tornado," Sally said.

"It's up to us," Eugene agreed. "I don't think Ms. Beasley's on a trip. I think Mr. Dooms locked her in a rocket and is going to blast her into space . . . if he hasn't already."

Sally and Charlie GASPED!

"And he's using his Mega Brain Sucker to suck all the knowledge

out of her head," Eugene continued. "That's why he keeps forgetting snack time and recess. He hasn't sucked up those parts of her brain yet.

"That means there's still time to find her before he empties her head and it's three, two, one . . . BLAST OFF!" Charlie cried.

"Where would you hide a school-teacher?" Eugene asked. "Or a rocket?"

"Well, there's the Sunnyview Planetarium . . . ," Sally suggested.

"Also, the public bathroom in Union Park," Charlie said.

"Nope. The perfect place to hide a teacher and suck out her brain smarts before sending her to space is . . . right here at school," Eugene answered his own question.

Of course!

That's where Super Dude fought Jet Janitor and his Mop of Destruction in Super Dude's Back-to-School Special No. 16. A classic.

"And if we find her, maybe we can get an *A* on our report cards," Charlie added.

"We're not superheroes just so we can get *A*s," Eugene told Charlie.

"We are superheroes because we want to do good things."

"An *A* would be a good thing," Charlie pointed out.

The school day seemed to drag on forever. But even forever eventually shows up when the bell rings.

Eugene, Charlie, and Sally met in the hallway, ready for action in their superhero gear. "What now?" Nacho Cheese Man asked.

"We need a map

of the school," Captain Awesome said.

"Kind of like the one over Nacho Cheese Man's head?" Supersonic Sal suggested.

"That's the fire escape map," Captain Awesome said.

"Yes," said Supersonic Sal. "And it's also a complete map of the school. Look at all those weird little rooms."

"Perfect for hiding a teacher! And a brain-sucking machine! And a rocket!" Captain Awesome realized.

Nacho Cheese Man pulled the map from the wall. "Let's go!"

They followed the map to the end of the hall, and then down the stairs to the basement.

"It should be right over here . . . ," Nacho Cheese Man said. "There!"

A dark gray steel door was in front of them. There was no window, and the doorknob was rusty.

Supersonic Sal tried the door. "It's locked."

They heard a rustling noise from inside. "Someone's in there!" Captain Awesome said.

They put their ears to the door and listened.

"It's Ms. Beasley," Nacho Cheese Man said. "I'm sure of it. Mr. Dooms is sucking out her brains!"

"But how are we gonna break down the vault door?" Supersonic Sal asked.

"I can use my secret formula canned cheese to dissolve it," Nacho Cheese Man replied.

"You have canned cheese that can dissolve a door?" Supersonic Sal couldn't believe it.

"Of course. But it might take about a thousand years." Nacho Cheese Man sighed.

"We'll already be past fourth grade in a thousand years!" Captain Awesome cried. "We need to use the Sunnyview Superhero Squad Triple Hero Bash!"

"The Sunnyview Superhero Squad Triple Hero Bash! Great

idea!" Nacho Cheese Man said, then added, "Wait. What's the the Sunnyview Superhero Squad Triple Hero Bash?"

"Something I just made up," Captain Awesome explained. "Now let's bash!"

The trio of heroes locked their arms and squinted their eyes—

because squinting makes everything look more dramatic. Then,
with a cry of "Sunnyview Superhero Squad Triple Hero Bash!" they
charged toward the locked door
and smacked into . . . the *school
janitor*?

CHAPTER 5

Where No Kid Has Gone Before!

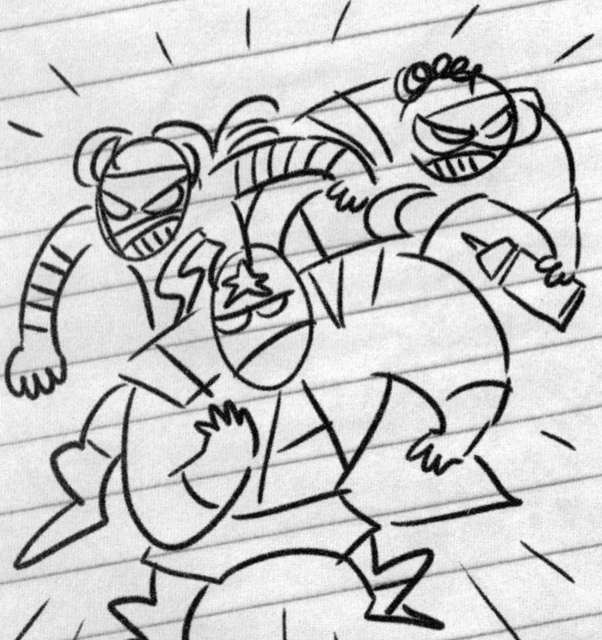

By
Eugene

Well, if it isn't Sunnyview's greatest superheroes!" the janitor said. "What brings you to the janitor's closet?"

"Any chance Ms. Beasley's in there?" Captain Awesome asked.

"Or a brain-sucking machine?" Nacho Cheese Man said.

"Or a rocket to blast them both into space?" Supersonic Sal added.

"Yes!" the janitor replied.

SUPER GASP!

The trio of heroes let out a super gasp!

"And here it is!" The janitor thrust out a mop.

"That's just a mop," Captain Awesome said.

"Or IS it?!" the janitor replied in a mysterious voice.

"Nacho Cheese Man took a closer look. "Nope. Just a mop."

"Or IS it?!" the janitor repeated in a mysterious voice.

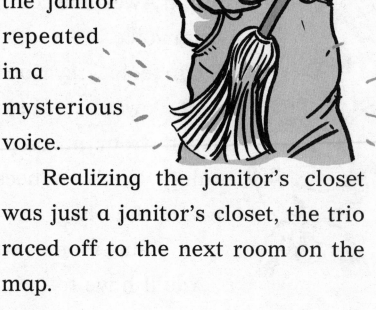

Realizing the janitor's closet was just a janitor's closet, the trio raced off to the next room on the map.

It was a plain wooden door. It wasn't locked. All they had to do was push it open.

BUT!

"This is possibly the greatest danger we've ever faced," Captain Awesome said in a grim voice.

"I can feel . . . my Nacho Cheese Powers . . . being sucked from my super brain!" Nacho Cheese Man said shakily.

"Supersonic Sal! You'll have to . . . go

on without us!" Captain Awesome stammered. "The grossness is . . . too gross!"

"It's just the girls' bathroom," Supersonic Sal replied.

"ARRRRRRRRRGH!" Captain Awesome and Nacho Cheese Man yelled as they fell to the ground and squirmed about like worms on a hot sidewalk.

"Boys." Super- sonic Sal sighed and went into the girls' bathroom to search for Ms. Beasley. She came back after a few moments to report, "No sign of Ms. Beasley."

"Must . . . get away . . . from the brain-sucking . . . Girls' Bathroom- onite rays!" Captain Awesome gasped as he and Nacho Cheese Man crawled to safety.

With the boys' superpowers once again at full strength, they came to the final door in the hallway. The one place that no kid, nor superhero had ever been before . . .

THE TEACHERS' LOUNGE! DUN-DUN-DUUUUUUN!

"You guys keep a lookout. I'll go see what's inside," Captain Awesome whispered.

Captain Awesome carefully

snuck into the teachers' lounge, but
nothing could prepare him for the
madness that awaited him.
**DOUGHNUTS! COFFEE!
MINI-FRIDGE!**

What kind of chamber of horrors have I stumbled into? he wondered.

RATTLE!

The doorknob behind Captain Awesome turned. Captain Awesome dove behind a couch. If he was caught in the teachers' lounge, he'd be punished with a lifetime of eating broccoli while doing math problems!

The door opened and in walked Mr. Dooms!

He sat at a table in the middle of the lounge, pulled out a notebook, and started to write.

By the elastic in my underwear! I bet that's a list of teachers he plans to add to the rocket and shoot into space! Captain Awesome thought. *Must . . . see . . . that . . . list!*

SNEAK!
CREEP!
CRAWL!

Captain Awesome wiggled along the ground like Super Dude did when he helped the Gummy Worms of the Gooey Galaxy defeat the army of Dr. Dentist and his mega Toothbrushers in Super Dude No. 312.

Captain Awesome slooooowly stood up behind Mr. Dooms, but

just as he was about to get a peek at the bad guy plans in Mr. Dooms's Bad Guy Plans Notebook, Captain Awesome felt a tickle in his throat. NO! It couldn't be!

AH-AH-AH-ACHOOOO!

Mr. Dooms, startled by the unexpected sneeze, looked up, but

Captain Awesome was already racing for the door like a spitball being shot from a straw.

Mr. Dooms has a Super Secret Invisible Sneeze Defense Alarm to make Goodness sneeze if it gets too close! Captain Awesome thought. He really is evil!

CHAPTER 6

Pepperoni Palace

By
Eugene

A kid's life would be one miserable dinner of kale salad and mystery casserole after another if it wasn't for pizza and pasta. That's why nothing made Eugene happier than pizza at Pepperoni Palace! Somehow, the sounds of loud video games and screaming kids having fun just made food taste better!

Eugene burst through the front doors wearing his favorite

pizza-eating baseball cap. *If you could eat a birthday, it would taste like this,* Eugene thought as he eyed the pizza platters that were lined up on the counter.

"There's no way you can mess up pizza. It just isn't possible," Super Dude said in Super Dude No. 222 when he fought the Aspara-Gross, who was trying to ruin all the pizza in the universe with his evil veggie pizza toppings.

"I want pepperoni!" Eugene yelled. He felt a little guilty for being distracted from the mystery

of Ms. Beasley's whereabouts. But then again . . . this was PIZZA.

"Waaaa-gaaaa-goooo-cheee!" Eugene's sister, Molly, babbled.

SHOCK!
HORROR!
CHEESY NO!

Eugene's dreams of pizza-mania splattered like a snowball hitting a roller coaster. His pizza joy was about to be crushed. Just like when you find out the "chocolate chips" in a cookie are really raisins!

MR. DOOMS was in the pizza parlor!

Ever since the Cheeseburger Embarrassment at Hamburger Haven, Eugene's parents didn't allow him to bring his Captain Awesome uniform when his family went out to eat. And now here he was, facing off with the dreaded Mr. Dooms, and all he had were breadsticks and dipping sauce!

Must send Mi-Tee Mind Rays to Charlie and let him know I need his help! Eugene strained his brain to send a message to Charlie.

"Hey, Eugene. Are you sending Mi-Tee Mind Rays or something?" Charlie walked up, eating a slice of pizza.

"Charlie! You got my mind ray message!" Eugene said.

"Sorry. My stomach's rumbling so loud, I didn't hear it. My family just came here for dinner," Charlie explained.

"Either way, I'm glad you *are* here. There's something you have to see!" Eugene said.

"If it's the new Mac and Nacho Cheese Pizza, I already saw it . . . and ate it. Deeeeee-lish!" Charlie said dreamily.

"No, Charlie," Eugene said,

turning his friend around.

Charlie gasped.

"Oh no! Do you think Mr. Dooms is here to sabotage the new Mac and Nacho Pizza?!" Charlie gasped again. "It's so deeeeee-lish!"

"Whatever he's up to, we've gotta make sure we're full of hero fuel so we can stop him!" Eugene pulled a slice of cheese pizza from a platter his dad was carrying. He took a big bite.

"Just like Super Dude says, 'Never fight evil on an empty stomach!'" Charlie gobbled his own slice.

But while they were busy chowing down on pizza, Mr. Dooms was headed out the front door, carrying stacks of pizza boxes.

"Mees metting maway!"Charlie mumbled, his mouth full of pizza.

"Mee metter mollow mim!" Eugene replied, his mouth equally full.

There wasn't a second to lose! Thinking fast, Eugene grabbed Molly's hand and raced for the front doors, calling back to his mom, "M'Im monna make Mean Minky Mants moo mah mayground!"

"What did he just say?" Eugene's mom asked.

"He said, 'M'Im monna make Mean Minky Mants moo mah may-ground!'" Eugene's dad replied.

"Yeah, I *got* that part," Eugene's mom said.

CHAPTER 7

The Ball Pit of Doom!

By
Eugene

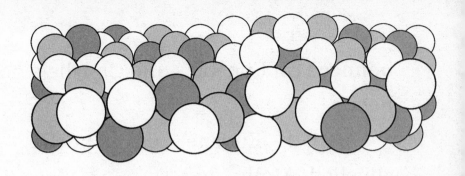

Is he doing anything evil?" Charlie asked.

"Not yet. Unless you count carrying pizzas toward a Little League field as evil," Eugene replied.

"Depends," Charlie said. "Are any of the pizzas veggie?"

"Waaa-gaaa-gooo-blaaaaa!" Molly squealed as she popped up between them in the ball pit at the playground. Colorful plastic balls bounced off Eugene's and Charlie's heads.

"SHH!" Eugene and Charlie shushed Molly, but it was too late. Mr. Dooms had seen them!

"Hey, guys! What's up?" Mr. Dooms asked, walking over to the ball pit.

GASP!

Eugene and Charlie

did the only thing two heroes without their costumes can do when a
bad guy asks, "What's up?" They
dove under the balls in the ball pit
and pretended they hadn't heard
Mr. Dooms.

"Hi," I'm Betsy McGillicudy." Eugene's mom walked up and introduced herself.

"Pleased to meet you. I'm Mr. Dooms. I'm subbing for Jan during her vacation," Mr. Dooms explained.

Eugene popped up from the balls. "*Jan*? Who's *Jan*?" he asked.

"Ms. Beasley's first name is Jan,"

Eugene's mom explained. She asked Mr. Dooms, "I heard Jan— Ms. Beasley—is out because she's visiting her family? . . ."

"Oh yeah . . . all the way in New Hampshire," Mr. Dooms replied.

"New Hampshire?" Charlie asked, popping up from the ball pit next to Eugene. "I thought you said it was New Jersey!"

"You're right, Charlie. My mistake,"

Mr. Dooms chuckled.

"He can't even remember his own story that he made up to throw us off the trail," Eugene whispered to Charlie.

"Gwaaa-maaa-gooo-baaaaa!" Molly squealed, and bonked plastic balls off the boys' heads.

"I know it's not easy being a substitute teacher. I hope the boys are behaving in class . . . ,"

Eugene's mom said hopefully.

"Oh, they've been fantastic!" Mr. Dooms replied. "You know, I coach a Little League team—that's what the pizzas are for. The boys should think about joining the team next year. . . ."

"So you can lock us in a rocket and blast us into space?!" Eugene accused.

"Ummm . . . no. I just saw you guys playing catch on the playground yesterday. You've both got great arms!" Mr. Dooms continued.

Mr. Dooms was watching us?! He's definitely planning to lock us in a rocket and blast us into space! Eugene thought.

Mr. Dooms grabbed his pizzas and smiled at Eugene's mom. "It was nice to meet you, but I've got some hungry Little Leaguers begging for pizza."

"Before you lock them in a rocket and blast them into space?!"

Charlie asked.

"Look out! Fly ball!" a voice cried out before Mr. Dooms could answer.

A baseball hurtled toward the group!

Eugene's mom gasped!

Mr. Dooms covered his pizzas!

Molly bonked a plastic ball off Charlie's face!

And Eugene whipped off his pizza-eating baseball cap and used it to catch the baseball.

Eugene smiled to himself and handed the baseball to Mr. Dooms . . . and then remembered that Mr. Dooms was a super villain and glared at him instead.

CHAPTER 8

There Is No Limit to Evilness!

By Eugene

Mr. **Dooms has been watching** us?!" Sally said in horror. "Ohh, there's definitely some evil going on here."

The trio huddled next to the cubbies in the back of the classroom for an emergency meeting of the Sunnyview Superhero Squad. Eugene told Sally everything that happened the night before at Pepperoni Palace.

"Okay, class. Everyone return to your seats," Mr. Dooms announced. "Time for a pop quiz."

"ARRRRRRRRRRRRRGH!" Eugene arrghed. "Is there no limit to his evilness?!"

"This is our last chance to prove Mr. Dooms is doing bad guy stuff and save Ms. Beasley before it's three, two, one, BLAST OFF!"

Charlie declared.

"Then it's time for Plan H!" Eugene said.

Charlie paused and scratched his head. "But, Eugene, none of us has a laser hovercraft driver's license. . . ."

"Or a laser hovercraft." Sally sighed.

"In that case, let's do what Super Dude would do if *this* happened to *him*!" Eugene squinted, because squinting makes everything more dramatic. "Put on our costumes and charge into battle like maniacs!"

BACKPACK!
UNZIP!
COSTUMES!

"Let's squirt some cheese!" Nacho Cheese Man pulled out two cans of cheese.

"My Super Lasso's ready!" Supersonic Sal added.

"MI-TEEEE!" Captain Awesome yelled.

"Oh, hey, kids, what's—YAAAA!"

Mr. Dooms yelped as the trio of heroes rushed toward him.

CHARGE!
SQUIRT!
AIRPLANE!

Captain Awesome whipped out a paper airplane of his own super design and threw it toward Mr. Dooms. As Mr. Dooms ducked under the

paper airplane, Nacho Cheese Man unleashed a cheesy double blast.

CHEESED!

It was a direct hit to Mr. Dooms's shoes!

Supersonic Sal twirled her Super Lasso over her head!

LASSOED!

The lasso
landed around Mr.
Doom's shoulders.
He spun about like
a spider trapped in a
nacho cheese web.

"Wh-what   are
you guys d-doing?!" Mr.
Dooms stammered.

"We know you kidnapped Ms.
Beasley!"Captain Awesome accused.
"Tell us where she is or we're taking
this straight to the principal!"

"What in the world is going on

here?!" a voice cried out from the back of the class.

Captain Awesome, Nacho Cheese Man, and Supersonic Sal spun to face this possible new threat, but nothing could have prepared them for who they saw standing in the doorway.

"YOU!" Captain Awesome gasped! "It's not possible!"

CHAPTER 9

Mr. Dooms to the Rescue?!

By
Eugene

It was Ms. Beasley! Standing in the doorway! And more important, she wasn't stuck in a rocket and being blasted into space! "What are you kids doing to Mr. Dooms?" she asked.

The class fell into a total silence except for a snickering Meredith, who mouthed the word "BUSTED" to Captain Awesome.

The trio of heroes stood wide

eyed for a moment, then the joy of seeing their teacher overcame them. "Ms. Beasley!" they shouted, then raced across the room and smothered her with hugs.

"Oh no! You're not getting out

of this one so easily!" Meredith shouted. "Ms. Beasley! I've been watching them! Captain Barf Face, Nacho Cheese Barf Face, and Supersonic Barf Face were running around like monkeys and causing problems like they always do!"

"I am afraid that's true. . . ." Mr. Dooms took the lasso from his shoulders.

A lump formed in Captain Awesome's chest.

". . . Because

they were showing the class the proper way to catch a villain." Mr. Dooms smiled and winked to Captain Awesome.

"Oh! How wonderful!" Ms. Beasley replied while she gave an apologetic smile to Mr. Dooms. "It's good to see you, Jan, er, Ms. Beasley, but we weren't expecting you until tomorrow," Mr. Dooms said.

"I came home from New York a day early because I missed my class so much," Ms. Beasley explained.

"New York?! I thought you said she was in New Jersey!" Captain Awesome said to Mr. Dooms.

"New York, New Jersey, New Hampshire, I knew it was a 'New'

state. . . . I just couldn't remember which one," an embarrassed Mr. Dooms confessed.

"Does this mean you weren't locked in a rocket and blasted into space?" Nacho Cheese Man asked as he wiped the canned cheese from Mr. Dooms's shoes.

"Of course not!" Ms. Beasley replied.

"But! . . . But! . . . But!" Meredith stammered, standing up.

"I think we've had enough disruptions for one day, Meredith," Ms. Beasley said. "Please take your seat."

Meredith crossed her arms and plopped back into her seat. Her face slowly grew redder than a fire truck covered in raspberry jam.

As Mr. Dooms and Ms. Beasley caught up, Eugene, Sally, and Charlie emerged from the back of the class in their normal clothes.

"Let's give Mr. Dooms a big thanks for the awesome job he did!" Ms. Beasley said.

The class cheered, and no one

cheered louder than Eugene.

"Sorry we thought you were a super villain," Eugene whispered as Mr. Dooms walked toward the door.

"Don't worry. It happens all the time," Mr. Dooms joked. "Keep practicing baseball, Eugene, and hopefully I'll see you at tryouts next year."

"You just might, Mr. Dooms," Eugene replied.

Charlie leaned over to Eugene and whispered, "Now I understand what Super Dude meant when he said, 'Don't judge a book by its cover. Judge a book by how many cool superhero secrets there are on the pages inside.'"

"And that's what makes Super Dude so much wiser than us," Eugene said with a nod. "MI-TEE!"

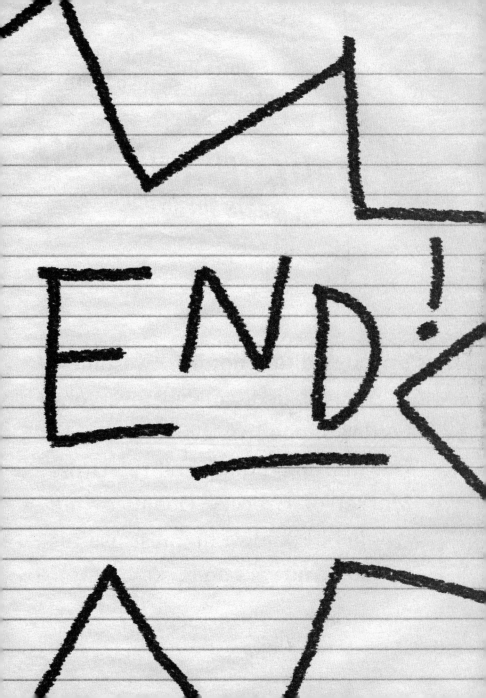

Don't miss the next Captain Awesome adventure!

CAPTAIN AWESOME
MEETS SUPER DUDE!

Eugene—aka Captain Awesome—is used to dealing with everyday battles of good vs. evil. Mr. Drools, Queen Stinkypants, and the Gross Market of Grocery Doom are all villains he knows he must use his awesome powers against.

But things have been different lately. There seem to be villains old and new . . . everywhere.

Then Eugene learns that there's going to be a Super Dude-tastic Super Party at the comic book store, and that Super Dude *himself* might make an appearance. Eugene is SUPER excited, but his awesome sense tells him something evil might be brewing, too.